This no

belongs to:

Made in the USA
Monee, IL
21 October 2021

80523066R00069